CW00919124

First published in 2012 by
The Puppet Company Ltd
Units 2–4 Cam Centre
Wilbury Way
Hitchin
Herts
SG4 0TW

www.thepuppetcompany.com

ISBN: 978-1-908633-04-0

British Library Cataloguing-in-Publication Data
A catalogue record for this book is available
from the British Library

Printed in China

Nursery Rhymes

Nursery Rhymes

Re-told by Sue Lockey
Illustrated by Sandra Evans

Twinkle, twinkle, little star,
How I wonder what you are.
Up above the world so high,
Like a diamond in the sky.
Twinkle, twinkle, little star,
How I wonder what you are!

Humpty Dumpty sat on a wall.
Humpty Dumpty had a great fall.
All the King's horses,
And all the King's men,
Couldn't put Humpty
Together again.

Baa, baa, black sheep,
Have you any wool?
Yes sir, yes sir,
Three bags full.
One for the master,
One for the dame,
And one for the little boy
Who lives down the lane.
Baa, baa, black sheep,
Have you any wool?
Yes sir, yes sir,
Three bags full.

One, two, three, four, five,
Once I caught a fish alive.
Six, seven, eight, nine, ten,
Then I let it go again.
Why did you let it go?
Because it bit my finger so.
Which finger did it bite?
This little finger on the right.

11 12 1
10
9
8
7 6 5

Hickory, Dickory, Dock!
The mouse ran up the clock.
The clock struck one,
The mouse ran down,
Hickory, Dickory Dock!

Incy Wincy Spider climbed up the water spout,
Down came the rain and washed the spider out.
Out came the sunshine and dried up all the rain,
So Incy Wincy Spider climbed up the spout again!